Fern Hollow is a wonderful place to live. Ask Professor Sigmund Swamp or old Brock Gruffy to tell you about their lovely little village, and they will talk all day and yet hardly have begun.

They will tell you that Fern Hollow nestles at the foot of the trees of Windy Wood and that through the village runs the sparkling ribbon of the River Ferny.

The animals of Fern Hollow are all good friends and neighbours, and if you are a stranger, they will make you feel at home in next to no time.

The Seasons in Fern Hollow

by John Patience

Published by Haddock Ltd., Bridlington, England
© Fern Hollow Productions Ltd.
Printed in Italy
ISBN 0 7105 0049 1

Spring

In Fern Hollow, as in other places, Spring is a time of great activity; a time for gardening, for whitewashing and for Spring cleaning.

It is a restless time of year when no-one can stand still for very long, but after chatting to you for a minute or two they will mumble, "I really must get that door painted," or "Dear me, it's May already, and I haven't planted my vegetables yet," and off they will rush to get things done!

It was Easter time and Monty was helping his Father, Mr. Tuttleebee, to repair the roof, while Spud and Heather played with their Easter eggs.

In the shop Mrs. Tuttleebee was wrapping some Spring flowers for Mr. Willowbank.
"They will be a nice surprise Easter present for Mrs. Willowbank," said the Hedgehog.

It was such a beautiful Spring day, and it seemed so stuffy inside the old school house that Miss Crisp decided to take her class out of doors.

The lesson was in arithmetic, which was usually rather boring (to everyone except Clarence Hoppit, who was clever at that sort of thing), but today, in the fresh air, arithmetic didn't seem too bad at all!

It was a fine day for the Spring Jumble Sale in the Vicarage gardens, and Parson Dimly, who was looking after the Lucky Dip, was pleased to see that lots of animals had turned up.

Mrs. Dimly took care of the refreshments, while Lupin had lots of fun on the Jumble Stall, which was filled with clothes the Fern Hollow animals had cleared out during their Spring cleaning.

Constable Hoppit was taking a walk with
his family on his day off work, when they
were caught in an April shower! Clarence
and Clarissa hurried along with their
Mother, while Constable Hoppit picked up
little Horace and raced on in front.

14

Then, under the shelter of the beech trees,
they all watched the rainbow while they got
their breath back, and waited for the rain
to stop.

In Boris Blink's Antiquarian Bookshop, Boris and his assistant Leapy were Spring cleaning, when professor Sigmund Swamp dropped in, looking for a book on Famous Toads.

"I think you will find one in that pile over there," said Boris.
"Dear me!" exclaimed the professor. "It would be like looking for a needle in a haystack. I think I'd better come back tomorrow when you've got the books back on the shelves again."

Mr. and Mrs. Rusty had taken
their cubs, Dusty, Rufus and
Redvers out to fly a kite in the
March winds. Rufus held onto
the line, while Redvers chased
around trying to catch the kite's
tail, but soon it was flying so far
out of reach that it was almost
touching the clouds.

Summer

Everyone in Fern Hollow looks forward to the Summer, to the lovely days spent picnicking by the River Ferny and to the visits to the seaside.

On their long summer holidays from school, the little animals go swimming and fishing, or play hide and seek in Windy Wood.

The bumble bees bumble around amongst
the wild flowers, dragonflies zoom low
over the river and no-one feels very much
like work, though of course there is still
plenty to be done!

Mr. Bramble the Farmer was in the middle of haymaking. The hay had already been baled and now Tugger and Madge were helping to load it onto the trailer. Little Tuppence was too small to help, but she had a cumfy ride on top of the hay.

In the middle of the afternoon, Mrs. Bramble arrived with lots of lovely things to eat and drink. Then the busy badgers stopped work for a picnic.

Professor Sigmund Swamp was retired and spent most of his time picnicking by the River Ferny. He had travelled abroad and lived in the tropics, and was not at all worried by the hot weather. In fact, he was heard to remark that he thought the Summer had been rather cool!

Mr. Twinkle's family were spending a lovely Summer's afternoon by the pool in the garden. Mrs. Twinkle was relaxing under the shade of a mushroom, while Mr. Twinkle floated pleasantly around the pool on an airbed.

Sparky, Dash and Skipper played around on the springboard, and Midge practised her diving.

The Summer was so hot that the River Ferny had dried up, and there wasn't enough water to turn Mr. Croaker's mill wheel.

"Never mind," said Mrs. Croaker. "We can all take a holiday until the rain begins to fall again."

"Hooray!" cried Lily. "Can we go to the seaside?"

"Yes, of course," chuckled Mr. Croaker. "And Dipper can sail his yacht in the sea!"

At the Railway Station Mr. Twinkle was having trouble with some foreign visitors who had lost their tickets. Fortunately the problem was soon solved by old Stripey, the Porter, who found them lying on the platform.

Meanwhile Mr. Rusty, the Engine Driver, checked his wrist watch with Mr. Prickles's and blew the Bluebell's whistle to warn the passengers that it was time to leave.

At the Jolly Vole Hotel, Mrs. Crackleberry and Poppy were serving cold drinks and ice creams to the guests at the outside tables, when Jingle's taxi arrived with the foreign visitors. Mr. Crackleberry picked up the Raccoon family's luggage and led them off to their room. Unfortunately no one had remembered to pay Jingle!

33

Autumn

Autumn is a beautiful time of year in Fern Hollow. The trees of Windy Wood turn golden, red and orange, and there is a wonderful scent in the air.

Unfortunately, the fallen leaves do cause
the animals something of a problem,
because they all like to keep their gardens
tidy. Of course you can always make a little
bonfire of the leaves, but it is best to check
which way the wind is blowing first!

Mr. Prickles had taken a day off from his job as a guardsman at Fern Hollow railway station, to gather the fruit and nuts in Windy Wood. The expedition had been very successful and, with the help of Mrs. Prickles and Polly, Mr. Prickles had managed to fill his cart so well that there was hardly room for another acorn!

Jasper, Patch, Tugger and
Monty decided it would be
fun to raid an orchard.
Unfortunately for them
P.C. Hoppit came by on his
bicycle and caught them—all
except for Jasper the squirrel,
who was very quick at
climbing up and down trees,
and managed to run away.

Dilly and Pud's Hallowe'en costumes were the best in the village. This was hardly surprising as their parents, Mr. and Mrs. Thimble, were the Fern Hollow tailors.

Dilly and Pud's friends were dressed in pixie or goblin costumes and some of them wore masks so that you couldn't tell who they were!

In the heart of Windy Wood Mr. Chips and his sons
Chucky and Flip were cutting down trees and chopping
them up for firewood in preparation for the Winter.

The hard work had made them feel very hungry and they
were all pleased when Mrs. Chips shouted that the soup
was ready.

One gusty day in October Lord Trundle was taking a stroll around the grounds at Trundleberry Manor when he bumped into old Blodger, his gardener, who was having trouble with the fallen leaves. Every time Blodger swept them into a neat little pile, the wind came along and blew them away again!

Mrs. Bouncer poked the baked potatoes
out of the bonfire and handed them round
to the children.
"One for Patch, one for Pippa and one
for little Toby," she said. "Be
careful, they are rather hot."

Mr. Bouncer lit a sky rocket
and it flew high up into the
night sky.
"Good gracious," laughed
Grandpa Bobber. "It looks
like it's going all the way to the
moon!"

47

Winter

Winter in Fern Hollow is more often than not very cold with plenty of snow. This suits some of the little animals very well. They can build snowmen, sledge and skate on the River Ferny.

But not everyone likes that sort of thing,
and some say that there is nothing
better than gathering a great big stack
of wood, making a nice warm fire and
maybe toasting a few crumpets.

Mr. Willowbank was a marvellous cobbler and could usually mend an old shoe so that you wouldn't have known it from a new one. But when Spike brought him Mr. Bouncer's Fireman's boots, he shook his head and said they would have to be thrown away.

"How on earth did your boots get such enormous holes in them?" asked Mrs. Willowbank.
"I put them by the fireside to dry," admitted Mr. Bouncer, "and they burnt."
"That was a silly thing for a Fireman to do," laughed Spike.

Jasper and Podger bustled excitedly into Brock Gruffy's shop. They had just emptied their Piggy banks and found that they might possibly have enough money to buy a sledge. Mr. Gruffy was very helpful and managed to find a super sledge at about the right price. Actually, it cost a bit more than the two little squirrels had managed to save, but the kind old Badger said that, seeing as it was them, they could have it anyway!

Mrs. Periwinkle could hardly believe her eyes; Mr. Periwinkle had forgotten to buckle up his postbag and all the Trundleberry Manor Christmas Party invitations were blowing away.

Fortunately Wally managed to catch up with the bicycle and Mr. Periwinkle came back to gather up the invitations. "I hope I haven't lost any of them," he worried.
"No one wants to be left out of the Party I'm sure!"

Fergus was all tucked up in bed suffering from a terrible cold.

"Not to worry," said his Father, Dr. Bushy.

"We'll give you some medicine and you'll be right as rain in no time."

"Yes, we must get you well quickly Fergus," said
Mrs. Bushy, "The Trundleberry Manor Party is only a
few days away!"

In the bakery Mr. Acorn was busy baking lots of delicious things to eat for the Christmas party. Jiggy watched her Mother icing a cake, while Jasper did his best to help by fetching and carrying. As for little Podger, it was long past his bedtime and he had fallen asleep on the floor!

And then at last it was Christmas Day, and time for the Trundleberry Manor Christmas Party! Everyone turned up (obviously Mr. Periwinkle, the Postman, hadn't managed to lose any of the invitations), and they all agreed that it was the best Christmas party there ever was!

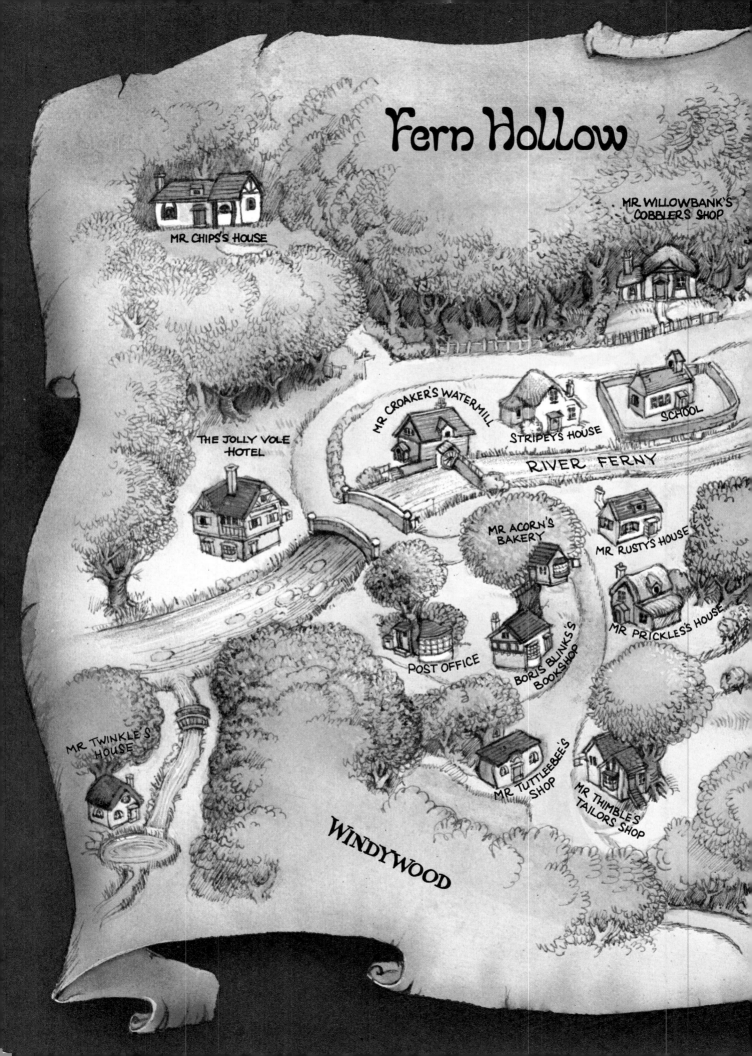

Fern Hollow

MR WILLOWBANK'S COBBLERS SHOP

MR CHIPS'S HOUSE

MR CROAKER'S WATERMILL

STRIPEY'S HOUSE

SCHOOL

THE JOLLY VOLE HOTEL

RIVER FERNY

MR ACORN'S BAKERY

MR RUSTY'S HOUSE

POST OFFICE

BORIS BLINKS'S BOOKSHOP

MR PRICKLES'S HOUSE

MR TWINKLE'S HOUSE

MR TUTTLEBEE'S SHOP

MR THIMBLE'S TAILORS SHOP

WINDYWOOD